D1015581

Apr 17

MOUNTAIN MISSION

# RACE THE WILD

## ARE YOU READY TO RUN THE WILDEST RACE OF YOUR LIFE?

Course #1: Rain Forest Relay

Course #2: Great Reef Games

Course #3: Arctic Freeze

Course #4: Savanna Showdown

Course #5: Outback All-Stars

Course #6: Mountain Mission

# RACE THE WILD

## MOUNTAIN MISSION

·BY **KRISTIN EARHART**·
·ILLUSTRATED BY **ERWIN MADRID**·

**SCHOLASTIC INC.**

TO MS. DENISE AND MS. MELISSA'S
CLASS AT SEVEN ARROWS SCHOOL.
THANKS FOR A WILD AND
INSPIRING TIME! —KJE

Text copyright © 2016 by Kristin Earhart.
Illustrations copyright © 2016 by Scholastic Inc.

ISBN 978-0-545-94065-8

10 9 8 7 6 5 4 3 2 1          16 17 18 19 20

Printed in the U.S.A.          40
First printing 2016

Book design by Yaffa Jaskoll

# CHAPTER 1
## THIN AIR, THINNER CHANCES

The tingling seemed to start in Russell's nose, but it also stretched to his toes and fingers. He clenched his hands into fists and buried them in the pockets of his jacket.

"I'm not that cold," Dev announced, looking at the rugged peaks above. Mountains rose in jagged steps, each taller than the next. The highest ones were crusted with layers of pure white ice and snow. "I shouldn't be cold, right? It's almost spring. So why are my hands numb?"

1

"The higher we go, the colder it gets," Eliza reminded them. "The Himalayas are the highest mountains in the world, you know."

"But that tingling probably isn't from the cold," Mari chimed in. "It could be from a lack of good air. As we go higher, there is less oxygen."

"Well, yeah," Eliza added between shallow puffs. "Obviously."

Mari was talking about altitude sickness. Russell knew it was no joke. Not getting enough oxygen could make you very sick. Russell's mom had told him about it after watching a movie. She had said that it started with a tingling, itchy feeling in the hands and feet, and it could cause dizziness and nausea. Russell knew that if he didn't feel better soon, it could sideline him. It could knock any of them out of the race.

"We've been climbing for a while," Sage said to the team. "Maybe we should take a break." Sage was the group's de facto leader. It was Russell, Mari, and Dev's sixth race with Sage. They all had come to rely on her. She looked out for them, and not necessarily just for their chances to win. But they all knew the truth: Sage did not like to come in second.

This was one time Russell did not agree with their leader. He preferred to keep moving. As long as he was taking steps, searching for safe footing, his mind wouldn't wander to other things. After all, there were a *lot* of other things to think about. It was the final leg of this round of *The Wild Life.* He and his four teammates were competing in a special all-star race against other winning teams from previous years. Some of the teams had already been eliminated. No one knew which teams were still in it, but Russell was willing to bet that his old friend Dallas and the rest of Team Nine had made the cut. Russell just had a feeling, and not necessarily a good one.

"Can you check the ancam again, Dev?" Eliza asked. "It's hard to believe we've hiked all this way and the race organizers haven't given us a single clue. It seems like a waste of time and energy."

Russell smiled to himself. Eliza was the newest member of their crew. She had once been their rival. Back when they were Team Red, Eliza had been on Team Purple. But now the five of them made up Team Ten, and they were working together in the All-Star Extravaganza.

"I just checked the ancam, like, two minutes ago," Dev assured them, patting the trusty communication unit. Dev kept it strapped to his chest in a handcrafted harness so he could grab it in two seconds flat. (One point six-three seconds, to be precise.) Dev took his job of operating the gadget, which was their only connection to the race organizers, very seriously.

"Can you check again?" Eliza prompted.

Russell glanced over his shoulder and saw Eliza scanning the rugged trail and gritting her teeth. At the start of the All-Star Extravaganza, the race organizers had forced each team to take on another member. Sage had drawn Eliza's name from a hat. Russell didn't want to think what would have happened if Sage had picked the slip with Dallas's name on it. He told himself not to think about it and focused on the rocky path.

After a moment, Dev answered Eliza. "The ancam still doesn't show anything except the *X* on the map. I think we should keep going. We aren't far." Dev glanced at the flame-colored sun as it dropped lower in the sky. "We might not be really cold now, but that'll change as soon as the sun goes behind one of the mountains."

"And spotting animals won't get any easier in the dark," Mari noted. After all, that was the whole point of *The Wild Life*. The race was an around-the-world competition—in some of the planet's most remote places—to seek out animals and animal facts. Russell knew Mari was right. She usually was when it came to the animals.

Nightfall would make tracking any wildlife more difficult . . . and more dangerous.

Russell took as deep a breath as his lungs would allow. "I agree. Let's keep moving," he panted. He was exhausted and needed to rest, but he wanted to get to their designated stopping point before he collapsed.

Over his heavy breathing, he heard a low howl echo through the canyon. Seconds later, another howl joined it. This one was long and high, like a siren.

"Is that what I think it was?" Russell wondered out loud.

"I believe so," Eliza answered.

Another howl carried through the cool, crisp air.

"On second thought, we should keep going," Sage said.

"Good thinking," Dev answered, with a hint of sarcasm. He picked up the pace.

"It's probably the wolves in a pack calling to one another, trying to meet back up," Mari said, sounding unconcerned.

"Or maybe they are warning another pack to stay out of their way," Eliza added in a matter-of-fact tone.

"Does it matter why they're howling?" Russell asked. "There are wolves close by. Too close for comfort."

"Don't be so sure," Mari replied. "Wolf howls can carry over six miles."

Six miles was far, but Russell was sure those calls were from much closer.

"I can see a light up ahead!" Dev called. "I'll bet it's our rest stop."

Russell searched the path in front of them until he saw the glimmer of a lantern. Then he looked back, past Eliza and their chaperone, Jace. He thought he could see the silhouette of a wolf on a cliff in the distance. Moments later, a mournful howl sounded, and Russell knew the wolves weren't far behind.

# CREATURE FEATURE

## HIMALAYAN WOLF

**SCIENTIFIC NAME:** *Canis himalayensis*

**TYPE:** mammal

**RANGE:** regions of the Himalayan Mountains in Nepal, Tibet, India, and Bhutan

**FOOD:** mostly small or medium-sized mammals, such as rodents and rabbits

Himalayan wolves generally like to work together and hunt in packs, especially in the winter when food is scarce. They prefer to hunt in the open, where it is easier to wear down their prey. In the summer, some wolves might live and hunt on their own.

Himalayan wolves vary in color, with most being tan or light gray. They often have white or darker shading around the face.

Scientists believe the Himalayan wolf is an old species, maybe old enough to form the base of all wolf bloodlines. The *Canis* genus, which includes the gray wolf, coyote, jackal, and today's domesticated dogs, began over a million years ago.

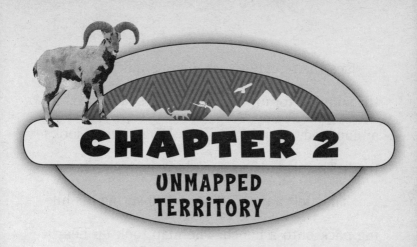

# CHAPTER 2

## UNMAPPED TERRITORY

The rest stop was a single room with a wood-burning stove on one side and cots on the other. In between was a long wooden table with two benches. It was small but clean. There was a sturdy door that would keep the wolves at bay. That was Russell's primary concern. Ever since the race had started, he'd had an odd sensation of being watched—or followed—and a howling pack of wolves only made him more wary.

Jace, their guide and chaperone, quickly located the supplies for dinner. "It'll be soup and rice," he announced, starting a fire. "Everything looks fresh. The organizers must have just been here."

"They left a map," Dev said, lowering his hiking pack onto a bench. The map took up nearly half the tabletop.

"It's a relief, seeing a real map again," Russell said with a sigh. "You know, one on paper. I can never figure anything out on that tiny ancam screen."

"Shhh. Don't call the ancam's screen tiny," Dev whispered. "You'll hurt its feelings."

The room fell silent, until Mari finally spoke. "Dev, even *I* don't think the ancam has feelings," Mari insisted, sitting down next to Russell so the map was straight in front of them.

"Maybe not," Dev said. "But it's our only link to civilization when we're on those mountain paths." His tone had only a touch of humor. Russell didn't consider himself superstitious, and he didn't think Dev would be, either. Dev was a tech geek who went to science camps. He probably preferred to stick to facts. But there was something about being high up in the mountains, surrounded by frosty peaks and frigid air, that made Russell feel vulnerable. Maybe it made Dev feel that way, too.

"Why'd we get a real map?" Eliza wondered out loud. "There has to be a reason."

"There is," Jace mumbled without looking up from the steaming pot he was stirring.

The five teammates gathered around the map, their heads so close they blocked out the flickering lantern light. "No hints from the ancam," Dev commented.

"It's all on the map," Jace added between sips from a wooden spoon.

"Well, this is where we are," Russell pointed out. Even though the faded green printing made the map look ancient, there was a small bright blue star drawn near the middle. Next to it were the words YOU ARE HERE. The star was in a narrow part of the drawing. It looked like a thin gulley between countless towering peaks, which were all white. "And these orange dots look like rest stops."

"So this must be where we're going," Sage said, pointing to a large red star.

"If there are all those rest stops, it'll take us

over a day," Eliza surmised with a shiver. She rubbed her thin arms.

"It doesn't look *that* far," Mari said hopefully. "A day and a half, maybe."

"Except there *are* a few mountains in between here and there," Dev commented.

"And more than one way to go," Russell added. "If we go this direction, there's a pass through these peaks, but if we head down that path, we'd go through one of these passes."

"Not again," Eliza harrumphed. "What's with multiple routes?"

"It doesn't seem like a fair race if the teams have different starting points," Sage agreed. "And on top of that, we can all choose different paths?" She hadn't liked it when the organizers had pulled

that trick in the Outback on the last leg of their race, and Russell knew she wasn't going to like it now. "All we know is that there are three other teams still in the competition. We have no idea which teams they are or where they started. It seems impossible for all the routes to be equal in distance and difficulty. How can they do that?"

Jace had started carrying large bowls and spoons shaped like small ladles to the table.

"Why can't the race go back to the way it was before?" Sage continued her rant.

"That's not the only change," Jace announced, placing the last bowl in front of Dev. All eyes turned to him as he sat down. "Since it's the All-Star Extravaganza, the organizers wanted to mix things up. The winning team won't just be the one who crosses the finish line first," he explained, stirring the soup with his ladle. "Now there's a point system. For this last leg, you'll get points for answering clues, and points if you actually get a picture of one of the animals. The team with the highest point total will win."

Russell watched Sage's eyebrows crinkle together as she scowled. After a moment, Mari took a deep breath and looked around the table. "This could be good, you guys," she said. "It's not easy tracking a lot of these animals. Both Himalayan predators and prey can be aloof and secretive. I mean, I want to see as much wildlife as I can, but maybe the point system will help us figure out what to go after."

An uncomfortable silence followed. "But it makes everything *less* clear. How do we know the best way to win?" Sage asked.

"We don't," Dev answered, his hand resting on the ancam.

Sage rubbed her forehead, her fingertips disappearing in her thick blonde hair. Eliza said what Russell was certain Sage was thinking. "I don't like it."

"Whether you like it or not, the race is on, first thing in the morning. What you've got to do now is eat." Jace had never been so straightforward with them. On the last leg, he had barely completed a sentence. He had let the team call the shots. Something had changed. Russell wondered what it could be.

# HOUSE OF SNOW

K2

CHINA

TIBET

ANNAPURNA I

PAKISTAN

NEPAL

BHUTAN

MT. EVEREST

INDIA

BANGLADESH

Fifty million years ago, India was an island. It drifted north, striking Asia. The land buckled, forming the Himalayan Mountains, the largest mountain range on the planet. The Himalayas extend roughly 1,500 miles (2,400 km) and stretch from Afghanistan to Tibet, covering parts of many countries along the way, including India, Nepal, and Bhutan.

The name *Himalaya* means "House of Snow" in Sanskrit. Many peaks in the range are always covered in snow and ice. After the Arctic and Antarctic, the Himalayas are the region with the third largest amount of snow in the world. When the snow on the lower parts of the mountains melts, it drains into several rivers, including the Indus, the Ganges, and the Brahmaputra. These three river systems provide a water source for much of Asia.

Mount Everest is the highest peak in the Himalayas as well as on our planet. The range also boasts many peaks that would dwarf other mountains, including the treacherous K2 and Annapurna I. The mountains' high altitudes mean the air is thinner. There is less than half the oxygen as at sea level.

# CHAPTER 3

## PRIOR PLANNING

**A**s they ate and talked, it was clear everyone had different ideas about which route they should take the next morning. Which one was safest? Which was fastest? Which gave them the best chance of seeing animals and getting bonus points? Even though they all had lots of questions, no one had any answers—or energy.

Team Ten eventually decided on a route that headed due east. It was as straight a path to the red star as possible. Dev pointed out that there would still be twists and turns through the mountain passes, but they all believed they would reach the finish line by the afternoon on the second day.

After examining the map's every dot, line, and star, Russell's eyes ached. He was too tired to speak. He didn't even remember lying down. The next morning, when Sage shook him awake, he was on a cot in his sleeping bag, still in yesterday's hiking gear.

"You like waking people up, don't you?" he mumbled with disbelief.

"Maybe," Sage replied, absentmindedly picking at her nail as she stood staring down at him. The room was still dark, with a dull hint of light straining through the curtains. "But I took it easy on you. I woke Dev up by telling him that the ancam was missing."

"It's true," Dev confirmed. He sat on the edge of his cot as he pulled on a red zippered fleece. "But I sleep with the ancam under my pillow, so I knew it was safe." Dev looked pretty proud of himself. "Anyway, Sage thinks you're soft."

"That's not what I said," Sage insisted.

"But it's what you meant," Eliza chimed in.

Now, *that* woke Russell up. He couldn't remember Eliza attempting to be funny before, but now she was doing it at the crack of dawn, at his expense. He didn't mind. It was part of being on a team, knowing everyone well enough to give them a hard time. He and his friends from home always used to trash talk on the football field.

"Come on, Russell," Mari said, as if she hadn't heard a word the other three had uttered. "Let's go check out the supplies."

There was a pile of gear and snacks under a tarp by the front door. Soon they were all stocking up, stuffing energy bars and dried nuts into every spare pocket they had.

"I assume you saw that there won't be food at all of the rest stops," Eliza announced. "This might have to get us through the race." Hearing that, Russell shoved more jerky into his pack.

"Prior planning prevents poor performance," Jace said under his breath.

"What?" Russell asked. He glanced over to where their guide was reorganizing his own bag.

Jace repeated himself, then added, "It was one of my dad's favorite sayings."

"What does that mean?" Sage asked as she moved a pile of snowshoes so she could reach a box of hiking socks.

"It means if you do a good job planning, you aren't as likely to make mistakes."

Sage dropped the snowshoes and stared at their chaperone. "I *know* what it means in general, but how does that apply to us?"

"You should be prepared?" Jace said with a shrug. Technically, the guides were not allowed to advise the contestants. Javier, their former chaperone, had always followed that rule, too.

"I'll tell you what it means," Dev announced. "We need to take climbing equipment. Ropes, carabiners, the whole mess. There's still snow and ice out there. Where the path isn't frozen it could be slushy, muddy, slippery. We need backup clothes, layers." He kept talking to himself as he began sorting through the equipment and supplies closer to the door. Russell joined him, making distinct piles.

"Fine. Figure out what else we need," Sage said, "but do it quick. The race starts again in fifteen minutes."

Sage headed to the bathroom. When she returned, she promptly put her hands on her hips. "How are we going to carry all that?"

"I think we need it," Dev stated.

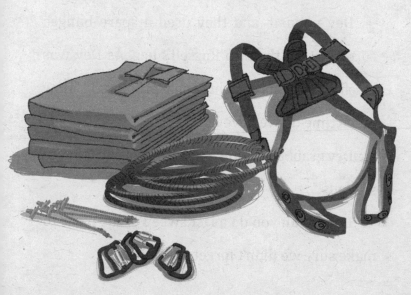

"We probably do," Mari said, joining the group, "but we should remember that we can't leave anything behind. Everything has to be like we found it."

"So no littering," Eliza said. "Obviously."

"My pack's at capacity," Sage said. "If I have to carry more, it'll slow me down."

"I can take more," Russell offered. "I can get those ropes. And some of the harnesses."

Dev nodded, and they used a spare bungee cord to strap them to Russell's bag. As Dev was cinching the cord tight, Sage prompted, "How much time do we have left?"

Dev grabbed the ancam and called out, "Ninety seconds."

"Eliza, can you do a last sweep of the place to make sure we didn't forget anything?"

Eliza trotted back inside and quickly came back. "All clear," she announced.

"And so is the team," said Jace, tapping his watch. "You're good to go."

"Okay, Team Ten, this is it," Sage said to make it official, and they all took off along the same path they'd taken the day before. "Dev, please tell us when we have a clue, otherwise we're just taking in the scenery."

"Will do." Dev had loaded a copy of the map on the ancam, and Russell had the real thing in a waterproof pouch on the inside of his jacket.

The sun was on the rise, cresting the top of a mountain and making the clouds a brilliant white. Now that they weren't scurrying around to gather supplies and secure backpacks, Russell realized he could see his breath. His headache from the day before was gone—no more tingling fingers or toes. But he still had that nagging feeling. He searched the horizon, scanning the craggy face of the rock walls. He even glanced over his shoulder.

"What are the chances that those wolves from last night are still on the prowl?" he asked out loud.

"Not likely," Mari said.

"You sure? I thought I heard something," Russell stated.

"It could be the snow melting," Dev suggested. "There are probably countless tiny streams trickling down the cliffs."

As the sun grew taller in the sky, light glistened on the melting snow. Russell avoided the chilly puddles on the path. Now was no time for soggy socks.

"We got it!" Dev called out. "Our clue!" He read it to the group.

Six legs,

Four wings,

Biggest of the big,

On its back—

Yellow-and-black,

And spring red

In its basket.

First thing in the morning,

Nests shiver with a warning.

# CREATURE FEATURE

## HIMALAYAN CLIFF BEE

**SCIENTIFIC NAME:** *Apis dorsata laboriosa*

**TYPE:** insect

**RANGE:** regions of the Himalayan Mountains
in Nepal, China, India, and Bhutan

**FOOD:** mostly nectar and pollen. Queen

bees eat a special substance called royal jelly.

The Himalayan cliff bee is the largest of all honeybees, measuring over an inch. The bees live in colonies and build giant disk-shaped hives on the sides of the cliffs.

For protection, the bees line up side by side around the golden hive. Instinctively, they shake their bodies in unison, creating a ripple effect. This shivering motion is a warning, discouraging anyone trying to raid the hive. These honeybees are not only the largest; they are also some of the most dangerous.

The bees collect nectar. They store the nectar where it is exposed to air. The moisture in the nectar evaporates, making it thicker and stickier. Over time, it becomes honey.

Building hives hundreds of feet high should keep them safe. But this honey is extremely tasty. Local villagers climb handmade ladders 200 to 300 feet (60 to 90 meters) in order to reach the honey. It is an age-old tradition—and a hazardous one!

# CHAPTER 4

## AN UNEXPECTED STING

"The clue's not as tricky as you think," Eliza said as they marched along the muddy path. "They're just trying to throw you off at the end."

"You mean the part about a basket?" Sage replied, brushing the hair out of her face. "Or the part about nests that shiver? Because they both threw me."

"And what's the red stuff?" Dev added.

"Seriously? How did you guys win the last

race?" Eliza huffed with disbelief. "You need to start with what you know."

"And we know that six legs plus yellow-and-black bodies probably means a bee," Mari put in. "And they've told us that we're looking for the biggest. Around here, that would be giant cliff bees."

Russell had to laugh. *That* was how they had won the entire race. Mari.

"But what about the red basket?" Dev reminded them. "That was the weird part."

"The basket is a special pouch on the bees' legs. They use it to store pollen," Eliza said.

"But the basket isn't red," Mari pointed out. "The red is pollen from a special flower that blooms in the spring and makes the most amazing honey. At least, that's what the video that I watched said."

"I saw that, too!" Eliza said, and the two started walking side by side, comparing notes.

"Well, you guys got that right," Dev declared, holding up the ancam. "It was worth twenty points, but we'll get thirty more if we send in a picture."

"So that's how it's going to work," Sage said. "We can get extra points for the picture, or we can keep moving and make better time." She kept talking as they made their way up a steep path littered with rocks. Bright green grass sprouted in new clumps wherever the sun could reach. "Jace," Sage continued, "is there any way to know how many points we get for finishing first? Can we figure out if we should try to get a photo or just move on?"

"I don't have any real advice," Jace replied. "They didn't tell the guides the details of the point system."

Sage needed to have a plan, even though they didn't have enough information to make one. But that wasn't how Russell approached things. He didn't need to win the All-Star Extravaganza. They had already won *The Wild Life* as a team of four. Eliza was the only one who had not been part of the winning crew.

But if they won again, it would mean more prize money. Russell had wanted to donate a bunch of his Wild Life earnings to his local rec center. The center was kind of run-down, but he loved it. It's where he played basketball, flag football, and baseball in the spring. And it was where he'd met Dallas and his other friends who had all ended up on Team Green in Season 10. Even after what had happened, Russell considered meeting them a good thing.

When Russell had told his parents that he

wanted to donate some of the money to the center, they had refused. "It's for your future," they had said. "Maybe for college." Russell had tried to argue, but it was no use. He trusted his parents. He knew they were looking out for him.

If Team Ten won the All-Star Extravaganza, Russell could use some of the money the way he wanted. He thought about how the rec center could get a real backstop for the baseball field. He wondered if he and Dallas and the other guys would be on the same team.

"Dude, what's up?" Dev asked.

Russell gave Dev a long look. "Nothing," he replied under his breath—breath that was much more even today, now that he'd adjusted to the altitude.

"You okay?"

"Yeah." Russell lifted his eyes from the ground to discover that they were nearing the top of a pass, a narrow path between two mountains. They had been in the shadow of a mighty peak, but now the sun warmed Russell's head, right through his tight curls to his scalp.

"Whoa," Eliza said as she joined them. The team gathered together to take in the view.

"Oh my gosh," Mari exclaimed, peering through binoculars. "Langur monkeys!"

"Where?" Eliza asked, cramming her own binoculars into her eye sockets.

Mari pointed to a clutch of trees thick with blossoms. "These guys hang out in trees and on the ground," Mari observed.

"The scientific term for an animal that's tree-dwelling is *arboreal*," Eliza added absentmindedly.

"What's super cool about these monkeys is that they behave differently than their relatives who live lower in the mountains. Up here, they cluster in a big friendly family group. Farther down, the groups are much smaller because the males always fight about who is in control."

"Why?" Sage asked.

Mari shrugged. "Mountain life is hard, so these guys stick together."

"It is hard," Dev said, studying the ancam. "Hard going. We're not making much progress."

"We've got to keep moving," Sage announced as she headed downhill at a jog.

Mari lagged behind. She couldn't just lope past the monkeys. Russell stayed back to wait for her, until he heard the other three yelling. Then he and Mari took off.

"What's the matter?" Russell called as they rounded the bend.

Sage, Dev, and Eliza were gazing up at a wall of red rock.

"Whoa, it's gigantic," Russell said.

"Well, yeah," Dev agreed. "But more importantly, look up there. Gigantic bees."

"No way," replied Russell.

"Way," said Dev. "We got lucky."

They all stared at the disk-shaped masses that jutted out from the cliff wall. The hives were humongous, and they were covered with hundreds of huge bees.

"There's even a ladder." Eliza motioned to an old rope ladder that was obviously handmade. It went hundreds of feet straight up.

"I don't know," Mari mumbled. She stared at the cliff and raked her teeth along her upper lip.

"I can do it," Russell offered. But Dev insisted that as the keeper of the ancam it was his duty.

The team approached the ladder together. "I don't know," Mari repeated. "It feels like we shouldn't."

"We're not going to get thirty points any easier," Sage said, and Dev strode to the ladder.

"I'll be careful, Mari," Dev assured her. There

was something in his voice—a softness—that made Russell think that Dev understood Mari's concern. The ladder wasn't theirs. They had no idea of its history. It probably belonged to local people who relied on the honey from the hive. The race's rules said they must leave the land as they found it. Maybe the ladder deserved that respect, too.

But the ladder was the only way to the bees, other than climbing the cliff and trying to get a photo from the top. While both ways were dangerous, the ladder would be much faster.

Dev steadied one foot on a low rung and pulled himself up.

"Don't get too close," Mari advised. "If you upset one bee, it will release a chemical that the other bees will detect. Then the whole hive will be on alert. That's all it takes to start a swarm."

"Well, thanks, Mari," Dev said, forcing a swallow.

When she thought Dev was out of earshot, Eliza whispered, "Too bad we didn't pack a bee helmet. I saw one back at the rest stop."

"Well, feel free to go back and get it," Sage replied dismissively. "Grab me an extra granola bar while you're at it."

Eliza locked eyes with Russell. When they'd first met, Sage hadn't had a sense of humor *at all*. She had finally developed one, but she didn't always use it at the right time.

"A bee helmet might have been nice, but there's no way I would have carried it," Russell said. "I already feel like a pack mule. Besides, Dev will play it safe up there." At least Russell hoped he would.

Staring up at Dev's lanky body, all knees and

elbows, Russell felt a surge of concern. He stepped forward and used his weight to steady the swinging of the ladder.

"Just a little farther and I can get it with the zoom," Dev called down.

But at that moment, something dropped from above. It hit Russell's shoulder and ricocheted to the ground. Before he could react, something else hit his arm with a decisive ping. Russell let go of the ladder to rub the spot. Whatever it was, it really stung.

"Wait. What's that?" Eliza asked. She motioned toward the hives with one hand and gripped her binoculars with the other.

"They're starting to swarm," Mari murmured.

A chill ran through Russell, numbing him. It was Sage who managed to cry out. "Dev! Get down! Now!"

# CREATURE FEATURE

## CENTRAL HIMALAYAN LANGUR

**SCIENTIFIC NAME:** *Semnopithecus*

*schistaceus*

**TYPE:** mammal

**RANGE:** regions of the Himalayan Mountains in Pakistan, Nepal, China, India, and Bhutan

**FOOD:** fruit, leaves, flowers, and buds

The Central Himalayan langur is a species of gray langur monkey that lives 5,000 to 13,000 feet (1,500 to 4,000 meters) above sea level. It's a mountain monkey! It travels up and down the mountain with the seasons, preferring lower levels during the winter and higher climbs from spring to early fall.

Langur bodies are long and slender, with hands and feet to match. They eat a variety of plant foods and have large, complex stomachs for digesting fruit, leaves, and other plants.

There are many different species of langur monkey. In India, some are even trained to chase less-friendly monkeys away from people's gathering places. These helpful monkeys are revered as a sacred symbol of the Hindu god Hanuman.

# CHAPTER 5

## A SWARM OF WORRIES

**R**ussell held tight to the ladder. When he glanced up, he couldn't see anything but the intense glare of the sun. From the way the ladder pitched and swayed, he could tell Dev was scrambling toward the ground. The question was whether a massive swarm of bees was coming with him.

Jace rushed forward and took Russell's place. Russell backed away and was at last able to see Dev, who was shinnying down the ladder rung by rung. Russell narrowed his eyes, searching for a swarm of angry insects. He didn't see one, but he did see something else plunge past them. *More rubble?* Russell wondered. He rubbed his arm again.

"What's going on?" Mari asked. Despite being huddled with the others, she had covered her eyes and hadn't seen a thing.

"He's got it," Sage answered under her breath, putting an arm on Mari's shoulder. "He's almost here, and the bees seem to have settled down."

Yet, just as Sage said it, they all heard a crack, followed by a hum, like the long vibration of a guitar string. The hum grew louder.

"It's one of the hives!" Eliza cried. "An entire hive! Run!"

At first, Russell couldn't move. A dark, churning cloud—a mass of giant insects moving as one—was headed their way.

Jace let go of the ladder and started to grab each of the kids, one by one, and hurtle them in the direction of the trees. "Go!" he yelled. "To the trees!"

Russell shielded his eyes. Then came a two-handed shove, and Russell stumbled forward, catching himself. "Go!" Jace yelled again. Russell got the hint and took off running. Then the guide pulled Dev from the ladder and together they ran after the rest of the team.

Under the cover of the thick leaves, the team gathered together and caught their breath. Russell took off his backpack and tried to stretch out his shoulders.

"What happened back there?" Eliza blurted.

"I'm not sure, but we've got to be on alert," Jace answered.

"What do you mean?" Sage asked, pressing for details.

"I mean that this isn't the safest place for kids to be plotting their own course," Jace confided. "It's wilder than other places you've been. The animals. The mountains. I mean, you can't even trust the ground under your feet. It's *always* moving."

Russell listened closely. Did Jace think there might have been a tremor, a small earthquake?

What Jace suggested made sense. Russell had learned about the Himalayas in science class. He learned that the tectonic plates under the earth's crust are in constant movement. In some regions, the plates move more than others. The Himalayas were one of those places. The plate movement could cause regular earthquakes and landslides.

"We're pretty much on our own out here." Jace wiped the sweat from his forehead with the back of his arm, but he kept his gaze toward the ground. "I trust you guys and all, but this terrain is rough even for seasoned hikers and climbers. A joyride, it is not."

Russell glanced around at his teammates. Expressions were grave. This wasn't just about winning the race. It was about surviving the mountains. *The Wild Life* had never been like that before.

"On the bright side," Dev began, "I got a shot of the bees, so we should earn the points."

Instead of cheers, there were nods of relief.

"And we just got another clue." Dev read it out loud.

```
No more red than Pippi,
No more bear than cat.
With rings and a mask
This mammal is all that.
The common name may make you
                  groan,
But now its family is all its own.
```

Instead of all chiming in to figure out the clue, the team looked back at Dev with blank faces.

Russell tried to focus, but his mind was still back at the cliffs, wondering what had upset the bees. Was it a tremor?

"Maybe we should try to figure it out as we hike to the next pass," Sage suggested.

"Yeah, let's do that," Eliza agreed, but no one moved.

After a moment, Sage pulled up her socks. Mari tightened the band at the end of her braid. Russell hefted his bag onto his back, and the whole crew ducked out from the cover of the trees into a dense, wet mist.

# MOUNTAIN FORECAST

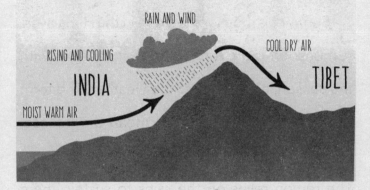

SUMMER MONSOON

RAIN AND WIND

RISING AND COOLING

COOL DRY AIR

INDIA

TIBET

MOIST WARM AIR

The Himalayas rise between the hot, humid land in northern India and the high, dry stretches of Tibet. The weather in these places is very different. As warm, moist air from India travels north, it gets trapped in the mountains and creates very extreme weather.

The wet air often clings to the mountain-tops, covering the area in a cloudy mist. At higher altitudes, where it is always cold, the wetness means snow and lots of it.

Summer is monsoon season in the Himalayas. A monsoon is a strong wind that changes with the season, and can alter the weather. The term *monsoon* has also come to mean the intense, enduring rains that come with the wind change. The region relies on the rains to sustain them throughout the year. Even though monsoon season can bring damaging rains and floods, it is essential to the people and animals who call the Himalayas home.

# CHAPTER 6

## TALLYHO

"This clue deals with misconceptions," Eliza said as they all made their way through the thick mist, one careful step at a time.

"So?" Sage replied.

"So, I think it's about misleading names. The clue writers love that theme, right?"

"Got it," Sage immediately responded. "Like how they bring up the common name at the end?"

"And then they say that the family has its own name," Mari chimed in. "They're making a big deal about how the animal is distinct, so it has its own scientific family name."

"Exactly," said Eliza. "Most animals only have their own species name. This one doesn't share a family name with any other animals. It probably doesn't have any close relatives . . . at least no living ones."

"I think I've got it," Mari announced. "Pippi Longstocking is known for her red hair, but we all know it isn't really red. It's not like stop sign red, right?"

"Yes," Eliza and Sage agreed. The boys just listened as they marched ahead.

"And we know this animal isn't a bear or a cat," Mari continued.

"Of course!" Eliza exclaimed. "The red panda!

Not really red, not really a panda. But it has a ringed tail and mask."

"Not a real mask," Dev pointed out. "Just super cool markings."

"Well, yeah, but it matches the clue," Eliza continued. "And this is its habitat."

"Go ahead and type it in, Dev," said Sage, but her tone lacked its typical authority.

Russell wondered if the fog was getting to them, clouding their brains. Or maybe they were still dwelling on Jace's warning.

"We got it!" Dev called out, his voice the only clear thing for miles. "The ancam also says that we got the points for my expert, death-defying shot of the bees. We'll get thirty more if we find ourselves a not-really red panda."

"In this fog?" Eliza answered.

"They're secretive as it is," added Mari.

"I'm just letting you know," Dev defended himself.

"Well, make sure you let us know when there's a new clue," Sage cut in. She glanced back at Jace, and the guide nodded.

"Will do," promised Dev.

The fog wouldn't let up. It only seemed to knit itself thicker as they climbed a steep path. Russell stumbled, his heavy pack shifted forward and forced him to the ground. Gravel pressed into his palms as he rested on all fours and tried to catch his breath. Jace pulled him back up by tugging on his bag's shoulder straps. "Geez. What do you have in that thing?"

"Stuff," Russell answered as he wiped the dirt and dust from his hands. He couldn't remember all the things he'd offered to carry. Now he was regretting his generosity. He grabbed his gloves from an outside pocket of the pack. Without the sun, the day wasn't nearly as warm as yesterday.

Russell and Jace hurried to catch up, listening for clues as to how much ground the others had covered. The team's voices and footsteps echoed back at them, and Russell wondered just how close the mountain walls were on either side. He hadn't heard any signs of the wolves, but that didn't mean there weren't other predators on the prowl. The pass seemed narrow, and Russell thought about how easy it'd be for them to get trapped.

"We got the next clue," Dev said after they'd rejoined the group. "Here it is."

Short gray wool that shields
from cold.
Short rubbery hooves to not
lose hold.
Dark stripe along the side.
On bare cliffs, nowhere to hide.
Fleet of foot on mountain face—
A fight for life is a race of
grace.

"Well, we should all know what that is," Eliza said at once.

Russell groaned.

"Tell us," Sage prompted.

"It could be any number of cliff-dwelling animals," Mari answered, "but there's a common species called the blue sheep that has a stripe along its side, on both males and females. The short hair is also a clue since many animals have much longer hair to stay warm."

"Exactly," Eliza said.

Russell missed the days when they all worked together to figure out the clue. He suspected Mari might have always known the answers, but she at least had allowed them to feel like they were helping. Now that Eliza was here, the two came up with the answers quickly.

"But you said it was the blue sheep?" Dev confirmed. "Are we sure that's right, if the clue says the wool is gray?"

"It's not really blue, silly," Eliza insisted. "It just sometimes looks that way in the sun. It's also more of a goat than a sheep. But you can feel free to send in the answer. Okay, Sage?" Eliza paused. Sage looked for confirmation from Mari and then responded with a brisk nod.

With that, Dev began to type.

At that moment, the fog shifted, and Russell felt a drop fall from the sky.

"Rain! This is good," Eliza said. But everyone else grumbled, even Mari. "We can kind of see now, and I'm sure we'll get a shot of a blue sheep, because they aren't endangered and they graze in groups. Easy to spot!"

The cold was so penetrating that Russell didn't feel it on his skin, but in his bones. It hadn't been as bad the first day they were hiking, but he'd felt increasingly cold as they climbed higher.

"I see lots of rain and rocks, but no animals," Eliza said after a while. "You don't think they've already headed farther up into the mountains now that it's spring?"

"That's crazy," Dev responded. "It's still cold. Why would animals go higher up into the mountains where it's beyond freezing?"

"It's just what they do. They've adapted to

frigid temperatures," Mari said. "But it seems too early for that. I'll bet they're still around."

Dev announced that there was another ancam message, telling them to get to the nearest rest stop for the evening. He studied the ancam map. "The path splits up ahead. We want to go right to find the village."

"But the sun hasn't set yet. It's still afternoon," Eliza replied. "We could search for red pandas or blue sheep for a little longer. We need more points."

"Wait, there's more," Dev said, stalling as he read. "This could be a game changer." He paused again.

"Well?" Sage prompted, striding over.

"It's a point tally of what we have, and what's still available."

"Finally," Sage replied with a sigh. The whole team crowded around Dev. He held the ancam out so they could all see the screen, but the type was very small. It was set up like a chart.

POINT TALLY

|  | CLUE | VISUAL |
| --- | --- | --- |
|  | earned / possible | earned / possible |
| BEES | 20 | 30 |
| RED PANDA | 20 | (30) |
| BLUE SHEEP | 20 | (30) |
| CLUE #4 | (20) | (50) |
| CLUE #5 | (20) | (100) |
| 1ST PLACE |  | (100) |
| 2ND PLACE |  | (50) |
| 3RD PLACE |  | (30) |

"It looks like algebra," Russell grumbled. "Super Extra Advanced Algebra."

"See," Eliza said. "The photos are worth more than the clues, and we've only gotten one. We should take the long route and try to get more."

"No, you shouldn't," Jace said, moving away from the group. "You received a direct order. The organizers told you to head to the nearest shelter. That's what you should do." He glanced upward, scanning the cliffs.

Eliza responded by zipping her coat and forcing her hands in her pockets, her movements sharp and quick.

"If you aren't worried about your safety, maybe you should be worried about getting a penalty," Jace suggested. "From Bull Gordon himself."

Even Eliza flinched. No one wanted to go up against Bull Gordon, the director of the race. He had wrestled grizzlies, and was as tough as they came.

Sage put her hand on Eliza's shoulder as they all started walking. "It's not just a race," she said under her breath. "We have to be safe."

When they reached the fork in the path, Jace stepped over to the left and blocked the uphill track.

"Okay, I get it," Eliza said. As they turned down the gravel road that led to the village, Russell was certain he saw a pair of horns poking over the ridge, but he didn't say a thing.

# CREATURE FEATURE

## RED PANDA

**SCIENTIFIC NAME:** *Ailurus fulgens*

**TYPE:** mammal

**RANGE:** regions of the Himalayan Mountains from Nepal to Central China

**FOOD:** leaves, flowers, and buds

Also known as the lesser panda and the red bear-cat, the red panda is not a panda, a bear, or a cat. However, it is about the size of a house cat, if that cat had an extremely long, bushy ringed tail.

With its peculiar markings and preference for eating plants, the red panda has long been of interest to scientists. Over the years, they have unsuccessfully tried to link the red panda's scientific family to the raccoon and other mammals that share some of its features. Now, the red panda has its own distinct scientific family, and it is the only member.

The red panda is a tree-dweller. It uses its exceptionally long tail for balance. It also wraps its tail around itself for warmth in the frigid chill of the mountains. Its red coat helps it blend in with red moss so it can avoid predators. The black under its chin and along its belly blends into the dark bark of the trees where it roosts.

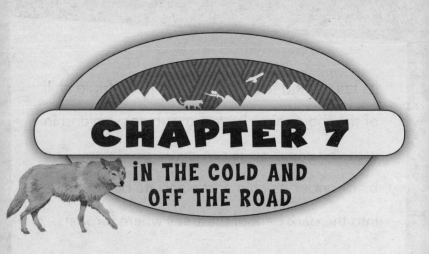

# CHAPTER 7

## IN THE COLD AND OFF THE ROAD

"**U**gh, why do I feel worse now than when we went to sleep?" Sage wondered out loud the next morning as she pulled herself out of her sleeping bag, one leg at a time, trying not to kick any teammates in the process. "I'm so achy."

"Yeah? You want to carry my pack today?" Russell asked. His back felt like he'd lugged a brick wall across the Himalayas, and then had to sleep on it.

"It could be because we slept on the ground,

with only a thin tent between us and permafrost," Dev suggested.

"It isn't permafrost if it actually thaws at some point," Eliza corrected Dev.

"Well it doesn't feel like it will defrost anytime soon," Dev retorted, his glare as frosty as the air.

"It's not my fault that we had to set up and sleep in a tent in the pouring rain," Eliza huffed, stuffing her sleeping bag in its sack. "And it wasn't my fault that there wasn't any room at the official shelter, either."

"No one said it was your fault," Mari assured Eliza. "We're just not morning people."

"You weren't any better last night."

The whole team turned and stared at Jace. When the guide looked up, he gulped. "Did I say that out loud? Sorry. I'm not a morning person, either." He turned back toward his bag and concentrated on stuffing his tiny travel pillow inside.

Russell knew what Jace was getting at. They all did. The rest stop in the village had been full. Another team had beaten them there. The cottage had looked warm, and good smells had carried into the cold air when the door opened. It hadn't been easy watching that door close again.

Even though there were other buildings in the small village, Jace wouldn't let them sneak in and take shelter there, even as the light drizzle turned into a pelting rain. He had said it was trespassing and against race rules. So they had to pitch a tent, and eat nut bars and jerky for dinner. No one had been happy about it.

"We should try to get ourselves together," the

guide said. "We need to finish this race today, or we might have to spend another frigid night in a tent without much to eat."

That got the group moving. They weren't anywhere close to the finish line yet. Plus, they had to pack everything, even the soggy fleeces that Sage and Eliza discovered in the corner of the tent.

"I was going to wear that," Sage complained.

"Well it's a good thing I packed extra layers," Mari said, digging through her bag for her backup. "You can borrow this."

"I don't suppose anyone can loan me something," Eliza said as she wrung the rainwater from her hoodie. Dev tossed her a replacement.

"Time?" Sage bellowed from where she was tugging a tent pole from the frozen mud.

Dev checked the ancam. "Two minutes!" he called out. Everyone tried to strip down the campsite as quickly as they could.

Sage's eyes narrowed. "We can eat as we go, folks, but don't let it slow you down." Now that the mist was gone, so was her lax leadership.

"And don't let it keep you from looking for the animals on our list. That's how we'll get extra points," Eliza reminded the team.

Before going to sleep the night before, they had examined the map by flashlight. The only bonus of not getting to sleep in the warm shelter was that they had hiked a while before finding a decent place to pitch their tent. Now they were farther along the route. Plus, Russell and Dev had discovered a new pass on the map, one that cut between two of the highest mountains. It was practically a shortcut.

The sun burst over a far mountaintop, and the sliver of light told Russell it was a good day for a hike.

"It's go time," Dev announced. "And we have a clue."

"Read it as we head out," Sage said, giving her hiking socks a final tug.

And they were off.

What could be more cute

Than a monkey's big, long snoot?

A peacock's colorful tail?

A tungara frog's deep wail?

A great large clownfish?

Maybe massive antlers are

your wish?

But for this animal to compete,

The male must smell smoky sweet—

A scent even humans adore.

They've worn it five thousand

years, maybe more.


"I know this one!" Russell was surprised by his own enthusiasm. He recognized the traits listed in the clue as ways animals attract their mates: fancy feathers; large racks of antlers; low, throaty calls. Almost all the things listed were features of the male of a species, including the answer to the clue. "It's the musk deer, and it's hugely endangered because people hunt it for the male's musk, which goes into perfume."

"So it's the male deer that makes the scent?" Sage questioned.

"Yeah," Russell responded, adjusting his gear.

"Sage, you got a problem with a dude smelling nice?" Dev glanced over at Russell with a toothy grin. The boys had taken the lead and had a good pace going. The path ran alongside the edge of a mountain. It seemed like it was carved out of the cliff itself, a steep rock wall rising on one side and an abrupt drop on the other. Russell was relieved that the mist was gone, even if it meant he could see just how big a plunge it was off the edge of the path.

"He's right," Eliza said. "About the answer. It's the musk deer. That's the good news. The bad is that they are extremely threatened. The chances of getting a photo are pretty much zilch."

"That's why it's worth fifty points," Dev said, looking up from the ancam.

"Well, no harm in trying," Eliza said.

"But don't forget that we also get extra points if we're one of the first three teams to the finish line," Sage pointed out. "There are only four teams left, so unless we're dead last we'll get something. We've made good time. Plus, the guys found this shortcut, so something would have to go very wrong for us to come in last."

"Um, what do you mean by very wrong?" Russell asked, coming to an immediate stop. He glanced back at the rest of the team.

"Like, would a giant rockslide completely blocking our shortcut, so we have to backtrack all the way through the village, count as very

wrong?" Dev questioned. "Because that's exactly what we're looking at."

"No!" yelled Sage as she took in the full magnitude of what Dev had said. A huge pile of rubble covered the path.

Russell looked up to the mountain on one side, and down to the sheer drop on the other. "There's no way," Mari said. "If we tried to climb over it, we'd just slide into a dark, dusty oblivion."

"That's just wrong," said Eliza.

"Very wrong," Russell agreed.

# CREATURE FEATURE

## HIMALAYAN MUSK DEER

**SCIENTIFIC NAME:** *Moschus leucogaster*

**TYPE:** mammal

**RANGE:** small pockets of the Himalayan Mountains from Nepal to China

**FOOD:** leaves, grasses, mosses, shoots, and twigs

Musk deer do not have antlers like most deer, but they do have extra-long canine teeth that grow so long they look like fangs. These tusks can measure close to four inches (10 cm) on males. During mating season, the males battle, using the tusks in their confrontation. Females have tusks, too, although theirs are shorter.

Musk deer are small in comparison to many deer. Their hind legs are longer and more muscular than their front, giving them a bouncy gait. They can manage high leaps, which allows them to escape many predators.

Only males have the musk sac that gives the deer its name. During mating season, the smell of musk lures the normally solitary females out of hiding. Unfortunately, the musk is appealing to humans as well, who hunt the deer for the waxy, smelly substance. Humans use musk in traditional medicines and fragrances. The musk is a rare substance and is therefore worth a lot of money. Gram for gram, musk is worth up to three times the cost of gold.

# CHAPTER 8

## ONE SHEEP, TWO SHEEP

"**M**aybe it was your buddy Dallas and Team Nine who snagged the shelter last night." Dev made the comment as Team Ten passed through the small village, backtracking to the path that led over the ridge.

Russell didn't bother with a reply. For one, he thought Dev understood that Dallas didn't exactly qualify as a "buddy" anymore. Russell wasn't entirely sure what his current relationship with Dallas was—not after he'd discovered that Dallas had put a tracking device on his backpack in the Amazon. Things tend to get messy when you realize your friends are cheating off of you.

"Hey, look!" Mari chirped. "Bar-headed geese! Those birds are amazing." Russell glanced over to where the head of a lake was visible in a valley, heavy mist floating over the water. If he squinted through his binoculars, Russell could make out a small flock of what looked like perfectly normal geese, except they all had distinct black marks on their white heads. "What they put themselves through to migrate over the Himalayas is incredible," Mari continued. "They hug the peaks, so they rise and fall in altitude. Truly amazing."

Russell couldn't believe Mari was able to get something so positive out of this hike, which, in every other way, was an epic fail. But he had to be impressed with the geese, too. While he no longer felt tingly, or like he was going to throw up at any second, the altitude still preyed on him. He felt weak, like he hadn't slept in days.

Dev used the zoom and got a picture of the geese *just in case*.

"Come on, guys," Sage said. "We can't give up. According to that list on the ancam, we've only got one clue left. Then it'll just be a foot race to the finish line."

"Shhh." Eliza hushed them. "What's that?"

They all listened closely. Russell was glad that it wasn't howling. Instead, it sounded like a clicking—a tapping.

"It might be hooves, clacking on the cliffs?" Mari suggested. At that point, Russell remembered the horns he had seen the night before, after Jace had herded them toward the village. They had finally reached the other path, the one that led up to the high pass.

"See, it was meant to be," Eliza insisted. "I *knew* we'd get photos if we took the high road. We need them to win this thing." Eliza started up the steep path. She surged ahead of the crew, until, all at once, she seemed to stand straight up, circle her arms, and fall backward.

"It's a tremor!" Jace yelled, bolting up the path to catch Eliza. The rest of the team crouched down, covering their heads. Russell felt loose debris fall from above, a layer of gravel and dust on the back of his arms and neck. When the worst seemed to be over, he gazed around.

"Thanks," Eliza murmured to Jace, who was cleaning dirt from his eyes.

"No problem," Jace answered. "And, so you know, I'm not going to stop you from getting a photo of blue sheep or anything along the way, but I have to advise you, as your guide, that we need to get to the finish line as soon as we can."

"I'm all for that," Sage said, sounding unaffected by the fact that the earth had just trembled right under their feet.

"Me too," Eliza affirmed. But Mari, Dev, and Russell all exchanged glances. While they shared an end goal of finishing the race, it seemed Sage and Eliza were still aiming to win.

Eliza stood and lended Sage a hand as the rest were still shaking clods of earth from their shirts. "Come on, Dev," Sage said. "Hurry up. Unless you want to loan me the ancam."

"Yeah, right" was Dev's answer, and he was

soon trailing them up the incline. Russell, Mari, and Jace followed suit.

"There they are," Eliza announced. The sheep were poised on shallow tiers of rock; the flock staggered up the face of the mountain. Both males and females flaunted impressive thick horns. Their coats, primarily a slate gray, had black markings along the sides and on their legs. Their underbellies were white. The combination of colors made for excellent camouflage. "And in this light, you can even see their blue sheen. We should get extra points for that."

"I'm not sure that's how it works," said Russell.

"I know it's not," Dev asserted, flipping through the various shots on the ancam. "But my killer photography skills deserve recognition."

"I recognize your skills." Mari patted Dev on the shoulder.

"As do I," commented Sage, "but I'd recognize them more if you'd just send one in."

"I'm sending, I'm sending," Dev insisted.

"And now we're moving, we're moving," Jace added, his tone a mix of humor and command.

After they'd been hiking uphill for about ten minutes, Dev had an announcement. "First, we got thirty points for the baa-baa blue sheep pic, thank you very much. Second, we have our final clue. Here goes."

```
How's this for a balancing act?
   Wide padded feet and a tail
          to match.
```

In these mountains there's but
one rule:
This steely stalker is the coolest
of the cool.

"We all know it, so you can go ahead and sub-mit the answer," Sage directed.

"Too bad we won't get a picture," Eliza added. "We could use the hundred points, but snow leopards are just too stealthy." No one argued with that.

"Sent and already accepted," Dev said. "The organizers are on the ball."

"That's good, just in case we need them," Jace answered. "Nice work, everyone, let's keep it up. Move on."

Russell heard the urgency in Jace's voice. Without another word, everyone sped up.

"According to the map, there's a path up here on the right," Dev said. "It's our best bet." But as soon as they came to the trail where they could turn off, they heard a call.

"What was that?" Mari wondered.

"Look," Eliza said, motioning to the sky. "A golden eagle. It was probably just that. A funny squawk."

But when Russell looked at Mari, she didn't look convinced. Then they heard the call again. It carried over a high ridge, from the opposite direction of their route.

"It's a person. No, people," Mari said. "It sounds like they're calling for help!"

# CREATURE FEATURE

## BAR-HEADED GOOSE

**SCIENTIFIC NAME:** *Anser indicus*

**TYPE:** bird

**RANGE:** populations exist in pockets from

Afghanistan and India, over to Myanmar and

Tibet, up to Mongolia and Kazakhstan, and more

**FOOD:** mostly plants such as roots, tubers, shoots, leaves, grains, and nuts; sometimes fish and insects

Named for the two distinct stripes around the back of its head, the bar-headed goose doesn't look like one of the world's greatest animal athletes. But looks can be deceiving. This species of goose is not all that large, yet it has wings that are especially long and wide, which help it fly at speeds of 50 miles (80 km) per hour. Furthermore, it is the highest-flying bird. During migration, it reaches heights of over 20,000 feet (7,000 meters).

At the top of the mountain peaks, there is about one-third as much oxygen as at sea level, and it is beyond freezing. The bar-headed goose has many adaptations that help it fly so high. They have special hemoglobin, the substance in blood that captures and carries oxygen around the body. Their hemoglobin is more effective, securing more oxygen from every breath. In addition, their blood vessels carry the oxygen-rich blood deeper into the muscles, giving the geese more energy to flap without getting tired.

# CHAPTER 9

## HARNESSED FOR HAZARDS

"It's coming from over the ridge," Jace said. "And that's a climb, not a hike. It'd be dangerous, even without yesterday's rain . . ." Jace's voice trailed off.

"Are we really sure we can help?" Eliza said. "I mean, it'll take valuable time."

"I just tried to contact the race organizers," Dev said. "But I can't get a signal."

Jace grabbed his own ancam and punched several buttons. "No luck here, either," he said.

They heard a faint cry again. The air swirled around, whipping over jagged cliffs. It was difficult to tell how far away the voices were, but it was obvious someone was in trouble.

"Well, I didn't carry all this gear for nothing," Russell said, slinging his pack against the ground. He loosened the bungee cord that released the ropes, then pulled the harnesses from the pocket. "Six in all," he said as he divvied up the equipment. Jace helped, holding the harnesses open so each teammate could step in.

"I should probably go first," Jace said. "Just to find the best path and secure the anchors."

Everyone tightened their harnesses and attached carabiners. All the teams had had a climbing tutorial before leaving the base camp, but Russell hadn't thought they'd actually do real climbing.

Jace thrust the first anchor into the wall of rock with a clank and a thud. "Once we're up over this ridge, the ground should even out a bit. Keep a good distance between you," he instructed, "to be safe."

Russell tilted his head back and tried to focus on the top of the craggy incline. He watched as Jace grasped a ledge and pulled himself up. He'd be next. Then Dev, Mari, and Eliza, with Sage at the back.

Russell had done the climbing wall back at the rec center, but it was nothing like this. Here, he had to find his own holds. He had to stretch his arms and legs wide to locate secure grips. His fingertips started to burn as he clung to a crevice, trying to find a place for his foot.

"Ready or not, here I come," Dev said when Russell wasn't even halfway up.

Russell was not ready, but he knew they had to hurry. "Come on," he murmured. The next stage was easier, with closer handholds and crevices. Soon he was at the top. Jace tugged him onto a ledge, his jacket scraping the jagged edge.

Up a few long steps was a hillside, still crusted with snow in places. Here the incline was less severe. There was a path that led to the top of the hill and then appeared to wind its way down the other side. While Russell waited for the rest of the team, he heard it again. The call. This time, it was clearly a cry for help. And this time, he recognized the voice.

"It's Dallas," Russell said, chills pricking at his skin. "It's Team Nine." Russell fumbled to unhook his harness from the others and began to scramble up the nearest path toward the voice.

"Wait, Russell!" Jace called out, but Russell couldn't wait. He was going to do whatever he could to help his old friend. He ran down the path to the cusp of a hill and skidded to a stop. Below, he could see three figures in orange coats. Even though they were far away—just orange-and-tan specks—Russell could tell Dallas was not one of them. Where were the other members of Team Nine? And Javier? And why were those three staring down the cliff?

Then Russell realized what had happened, and he knew he couldn't do anything by himself. He needed his team.

It wasn't as hard to convince them as he had thought. Even though they were in a race, everyone agreed they had to help. After all, they could have been the ones caught in a rockslide. Russell tried not to think of how serious things could be.

"We're coming," Russell called. "Hold tight."

Then Team Ten began their descent, rappeling down the cliff just above where the three members of Team Nine were gathered. With Jace as the anchor up top, they lowered themselves, their legs in front of them, walking backward down the mountain. "One step at a time," Jace said.

Even Mari, who was afraid of heights, trusted the harness as she lowered herself with easy, regular steps.

When Team Ten finally arrived, it was Sage and Eliza who went over to talk to the three members of Team Nine who were on the path. "Let me look," Jace said to the others. He went to the ledge and knelt down and peered over the side. "Javier, are you down there?"

"Jace, is that you?" Javier called up. Their former guide's voice was familiar but fraught. "Thank goodness. I'm not sure how much longer these rocks are going to hold."

Russell eased toward the edge and surveyed the situation. A swallow caught in his throat when he saw Dallas and another kid both crouched over, loose rubble under their hands and knees. The bits of ruptured rock looked like they could slide down the mountain at any moment. Javier was standing with one foot on a large boulder and the other propped on the cliff wall.

"Russell, can you guys get the ropes and a couple harnesses?" Jace prompted. "We're going to get them up." Russell did not respond for a moment. He couldn't take his eyes off Dallas, hunched over. Slowly, Dallas lifted his head.

Russell pressed his lips together and nodded

at his friend. "Yeah," he said. "We're going to get you up." Dallas and Russell's eyes locked. It was hard for Russell to look away.

Jace lowered the harnesses and the rope to Dallas first. Russell held his breath as Dallas shifted all his weight to his knees and began to pull on the harness and thread the climbing rope. A chunk of loose ground collapsed, tumbling downward. Russell watched the dirt as it skidded, until it dropped into the thin air.

"Ready," Dallas called. His knot looked secure.

"Keep your arms down. It'll give me more leverage," Jace directed. Russell stood behind him, holding the rope. The rest of Team Ten grabbed the remaining rope as an anchor.

As soon as Dallas's hands and elbows appeared on the crusty ledge, Russell rushed forward and dragged him onto firm ground. Russell only had a moment to hug his friend before they were scrambling to get him out of the harness so they could send it down to his teammates.

"Thanks, man," Dallas said, his voice breaking. "I knew I could count on you."

Dallas returned to his other teammates and waited. Russell had hardly noticed them, and now was not the time for introductions. There were still two people stranded below.

The mood started to change when the remaining racer, a redhead named Allison, was brought up safely. She was scraped and grimy but flush with relief. Then the rest of Team Ten concentrated on getting Javier back on solid ground. Everyone was surprised when the members of Team Nine weren't there to greet their guide.

"Where's the rest of your team?" Eliza's tone was full of disgust as Dev and Dallas appeared up from behind a big boulder.

"What do you mean?" Dallas asked, looking around.

"Your teammates took off," Sage said. Dallas looked as surprised as the rest of them.

"That's crazy," Javier insisted, pressing his hands to his face. "I mean, Allison was two loose pebbles from plummeting four thousand feet."

"You should probably go after them," Jace said to Javier. "Team Ten, we have to clean up."

"Seriously?" Eliza mumbled, but she got to work. Russell started to pick up the carabiners and extra harnesses, and tried to figure out what had happened. Where had Dev and Dallas gone? And why would Team Nine have just taken off?

The girls helped gather the gear. Sage stuffed the long climbing rope in her backpack. When they were done, Russell looked up and realized that Dallas was gone. He and Javier had left without saying good-bye.

"Your buddy said he'd see you at the finish line," Dev told him.

"Oh, he did, did he?" Russell heaved his hiking bag onto his back.

"He did," Dev told Russell. Then he shifted his gaze to the team as a whole. "So, everyone was okay. That's good, right?"

"Yeah," the teammates mumbled, uncertain what Dev was getting at. "What's not so good is that we still have no ancam signal. And now we have no map."

Jace grabbed his ancam and jabbed at all the buttons. "So not good," he said.

"Well, I've got the real map, the paper one," Russell said, unzipping the inside pocket on his jacket.

"Thank goodness!" Sage exalted as Russell unfolded the map. The team quickly huddled around him to study it.

"What if we go that way?" Dev asked. "It looks like we'll hit a more direct trail. And hopefully a safer one."

"Are you sure? Because Team Nine went the other way," Eliza pointed out.

"It does look shorter," Mari admitted, "but maybe the terrain is rougher."

"I think we can take it," Sage said. "Let's try Dev's route."

"Um, it's not *my* route. It has to be *our* route. We should all agree." The others all nodded with apprehensive murmurs.

"We'll make it work," Eliza asserted.

"Let's finish this race," said Sage, sounding more determined than ever. She slapped Eliza on the back and took off at a quick clip.

# CREATURE FEATURE

## SNOW LEOPARD

**SCIENTIFIC NAME:** *Panthera uncia*

**TYPE:** mammal

**RANGE:** high mountains of Central Asia

**FOOD:** blue sheep, ibex, marmots, hares, and game birds; occasionally livestock

The snow leopard has adapted to its chilly mountain home. This cat's short front legs and small ears make its body more compact, so it loses less heat. The snow leopard's hair is long and thick. It molts, or sheds, twice a year, with its winter coat growing longer and thicker, up to twice the length of its summer coat. Compared to other cats, the openings in its nose—or nasal cavities—are thinner, which warms cold mountain air more quickly as it travels to the snow leopard's lungs.

Its hind legs are long and powerful, to boost its body in athletic leaps. The snow leopard can bound six times its body length as it chases prey on the rugged cliffs. With large padded paws, it has incredibly sure footing. Its tail, which more than doubles the cat's length, provides balance . . . and acts as a cozy barrier from the bitter cold.

# CHAPTER 10
## SURPRISE SILENT STALKER SIGHTING

Like a drill sergeant, Sage had them moving at breakneck speed. They wound around peaks, going up trying inclines, until the trail opened up into a wide valley. It wasn't the best time for conversation, but that didn't stop Eliza from asking Dev for ancam updates every five minutes.

But the ancam still wasn't getting a signal. They stopped a couple times to consult the paper map and confirm they were on track. The closer they got to the finish line, the harder Sage pushed them.

No one bothered to talk about how they had helped Team Nine escape a deadly situation, and then Team Nine had deserted them.

Russell wondered what had happened. Did Team Nine really want to win that badly? And why hadn't Dallas gone with them? From previous experience, Russell knew that Dallas was willing to take risks to win. But his old friend had stuck around . . . at least for a while. Long enough to chat with Dev—and wait for Javier.

"I see it! I see it!" Eliza cried and clapped at the same time. "The Wild Life balloon is over there!" High in the sky, a single large balloon marked the end of their journey. Festive banners with cloth triangles were strung between the staff tents and up a tall pole. After three days of hiking up and down mountains, it was hard to believe they were almost finished. "Keep your eyes out for a last-minute red panda. We could use the points!"

Despite all his sports training, Russell was already winded. He had never worked out wearing a forty-pound backpack! As they hurried downhill, Russell could hear Sage and Eliza tallying their points.

The way Russell saw it, they couldn't change anything now. Either their team would have the most points or they wouldn't. As they neared the finish line, it looked like they wouldn't. Two teams had already arrived. Just as Team Ten was about to cross under the banner, Dev pulled out the ancam again. "Still no signal," he said with a frown.

"Don't worry about it now," Russell told him. "We're here. We made it." As soon as he'd crossed the finish line, Russell yanked the hiking pack from his shoulder and let it drop to the ground. Then he sat on the bag and drained his water bottle, not caring when the water splashed out and streamed down his face. He stared at Dev, who was dripping with sweat. Russell couldn't figure out why his teammate hadn't done the same. Mari lifted her braid off her back and fanned her neck.

Dev glanced around. Sage and Eliza had already approached the other teams, trying to find out if anyone knew the standings.

"I'm going to tell the organizers about our ancam, just so they know," Dev explained. Russell watched as Dev headed over to where Bull Gordon was standing. After a few minutes, he returned to the team with a smile on his face.

"Where's the ancam?" Russell asked.

"I had to turn it in," Dev said. "They had to make sure that the problem was on their end."

"And?" Mari asked.

"Of course it was," Dev replied. "Our ancam was as good as gold."

Russell wasn't sure why Dev was making such a big deal out of it. The ancam hadn't lost the signal until after they'd submitted their answers and photos. But Russell wouldn't pretend to understand any part of the special relationship between Dev and that device.

At last Team Nine crossed the finish line. Russell wasn't sure how Team Ten had managed to beat them. Was the route Dev had suggested really that much shorter, or had Team Nine gone off to track down last-minute photo points? Russell couldn't know for sure. He glanced over at Dallas, whose smile looked especially bright against his mud-caked skin.

Bull Gordon and the organizers herded the teams together. Bull climbed up on a boulder that was in the middle of the camp and cleared his throat.

"Remember, with the thirty points for third place, we've got 190," Eliza announced in a whisper to the rest of their team. "That hardly seems like a winning score, but I'm crossing my fingers anyway." Mari raised her hand to show that her fingers were crossed, too.

"Knowing a lot about wildlife doesn't always translate into knowing a lot about people—or caring." Bull Gordon glanced around the group. "I've watched you all through two entire competitions. If there were a way to earn points for taking care of not only the natural world around us, but also each other, you would all be winners. But that isn't how this race works." Bull's expression was serious. "And even though you can't get points for being helpful or thoughtful or kind, I noticed many of you doing those things. So I commend you." He reached up and touched the rim of his faded fedora, nodding to the group in general, but Russell thought that his gaze lingered on Team Ten.

When Bull paused, the silence was filled with sighs. Russell couldn't blame anyone. They were all exhausted. They'd been on their feet for hours . . . days. And all anyone really wanted to hear was who had won.

"Now it's time to announce the results," Bull said. His booming voice had brightened, and it carried up into the mountain air. "We have a runner-up with 260 points, boosted by the one hundred points for a snow leopard sighting. Team Nine!" Murmurs filled the crowd.

"How did they get that photo?" Eliza muttered, disenchanted.

"And our winners, with 290 points, also with

a snow leopard sighting, are the members of Team Ten."

"What?" The members of Team Ten shared a collective gasp. A snow leopard? When? Where? They were all mystified. All except Dev, who had taken the picture.

"Just go up and get your medals," Dev directed, giving his teammates gentle shoves. "I'll explain later."

"You'd better," said Sage, who had a big, fake smile plastered on her face as she threaded her way toward where Bull Gordon stood on the boulder.

Accepting the winners' medals did not feel real to Russell—especially since Dev was the only one who knew exactly how they'd won.

When Russell looked out at the small crowd, he saw Jace, who looked only a little surprised and very proud. And he saw Dallas, who looked pretty much the same. It made a lot more sense when Dev told them the full story ten minutes later.

"It happened really fast," he said. "When you guys were helping Javier, Dallas showed me the snow leopard. It had been pacing on the cliff above us the whole time. Team Nine had tracked it there. Then, as soon as I got the shot, it vanished, so I couldn't show him to you. And I didn't want to tell you about the photo, because I couldn't submit it without the ancam signal."

"And you didn't know if they'd accept it, if you hadn't sent it in during the race," Russell pieced together.

"Exactly. I didn't want to get your hopes up if

it wasn't going to count. I'm really sorry I didn't tell you guys," Dev said, looking forlorn. "I just didn't want to let you down."

"Um, you didn't let us down," Eliza replied. "You won it for us, Dev!"

"I would have liked to have seen the snow leopard," Mari admitted, her voice quiet, "but I suppose I'll forgive you, just this once."

"So let me get this right," Sage said, glancing over her shoulder to make sure the team was alone. "Dallas pulled you aside, showed you the fabulous one-hundred-point animal, and that was that?"

"That was that," Dev confirmed. "And then we won."

"We won!" Eliza called out as if reminding herself.

But in that moment, winning wasn't what mattered most to Russell. If there was one thing that he was sure of after trekking through the land of the mighty mountains and shaky ground, it was that solid friendships were game changers—and even lifesavers, sometimes.

He and Dallas might have had a rocky past, but Russell knew he cared for his friend. They had learned that they could trust each other when it mattered most, and Russell wouldn't let that change. He looked forward to taking the football field with Dallas at the rec center. It'd feel good to be on the same team again.

And as for his Wild Life team, it felt weird that he'd be going back to his real life where he didn't have all of them by his side. He was now accustomed to having each of them around. He'd grown to rely on their strengths. Sage's leadership. Dev's tech savvy. Mari's quiet kindness (and animal genius!). Eliza's ambition. And yet he'd miss them for so much more.

Russell had to remind himself that at one point, he had felt like he was stuck with this group of strangers. He had believed that all of his friends were on another team. Not anymore. Now Russell realized that their ragtag crew didn't make a good team because they were friends. But they were now good friends, and it was all because they had learned together what it took to make a good team.